Hot Streak

and other sports stories

by

Vaughan Webb

Watermill Press

Printed in the United States of America

Illustrations by Thomas Heggie

ISBN 0-89375-773-X

Contents

The Star-Maker

Scott took off his helmet. He was grinning from ear to ear. He had just scored another touchdown — his third in this game. The final seconds ticked away. At last, the game was over. The Tigers had won again. And, as always, Scott had been the star.

"Great game, Scott!" said Lew. Lew was a lineman. He played tackle in front of Scott.

"My best ever," Scott said. Scott was the star halfback. He carried the ball through the line. And he did all the scoring.

The team headed for the locker room. Many people shook Scott's hand along the way. He felt great. *I really am a star,* he thought. *I'll be a pro one day.*

Inside, the coach praised the team. "Everyone looked good today," he said. "But don't get too proud. Our toughest game is next week. The Bulldogs hate to lose. They'll give us a rough match. We'll have to practice harder this week."

The coach meant what he said. The team worked out every day. They were ready for the Bulldogs that Friday.

All the players were excited. They ran

out onto the field. And the crowd cheered. They yelled louder when Scott came out. He waved to the sidelines. A man from the paper took pictures.

Then it was time to play. The Bulldogs kicked off. On the first down, Scott was given the ball. Lew opened up a big hole. The halfback ran through it. No one touched him. He raced down the field. Then he cut to the left. Three boys were on his heels, but Scott sped away. He crossed the goal line. And he held the ball above his head.

The crowd went wild. Scott rushed to the bench. His teammates slapped his back. "Good work," the coach said.

This will be simple, Scott thought. *I'm too quick for that team.*

The Bulldogs watched for the long run. But the halfback kept scoring. He ran easily through the Bulldog line. By

Lew opened up a big hole, and Scott ran through it.

half time, he had scored three touchdowns. He was having a great day. But the Bulldogs had not quit.

Scott started the next half with another long sprint. The quarterback gave him the ball. Scott tucked it under his arm. He looked ahead. Lew had opened another huge gap. Scott charged through and gained ten yards.

Quickly, Scott returned to the huddle. Then he saw Lew. The lineman had hurt his knee and was limping to the bench. The coach sent in a substitute.

Scott was eager to run again. The quarterback made the call. Scott took the hand-off and turned. This time, there was no hole. The Bulldogs were all over him. They dragged the halfback down.

The Tigers tried the same play. Scott was thrown for a big loss. He couldn't

The ball slipped from Scott's hands.

understand it. On his next carry, he was hit hard. The ball slipped from his hands. A Bulldog scooped it up. He ran in for a touchdown.

The Tigers got the ball again. But they couldn't move it. Scott was stopped cold each time. His team had to punt. The Bulldogs were coming back strong. Before long, the score was tied. And the clock was running out.

Scott didn't know what to do. The fans were all quiet. They smelled a loss in the air.

The coach called a time-out. The team gathered around him. "This is it," he said. "If we move now, we'll break their spirit. Go at them hard."

Slowly, Scott walked back out. He had already lost hope. He was sore from being tackled. Then he heard footsteps behind him.

"Come on. Let's go," someone said. It was Lew. His knee felt much better. The coach had sent him back in.

At once, Scott's hopes swelled. "Let's do it!" he cried.

The ball was on the thirty-yard line. The quarterback called the signals. He took the snap, then dropped back to pass. But it was a fake. He tossed the ball to the halfback. Scott roared at the line. Lew opened up a path, and Scott shot through it. He gained six yards on the down.

Play after play, the Tigers marched downfield. Lew made the holes. And Scott popped through them.

The Tigers were ten yards from scoring. Everyone knew who would get the ball. The Bulldogs were waiting. Scott took the hand-off. He thought he would meet a wall of players. But Lew had blasted out a wide hole. Scott scored on his feet. No one had even touched him.

His teammates jumped all over him. The fans screamed in the stands. The game was over.

The Tigers lifted their hero. They put Scott on their shoulders. He smiled weakly. But he did not look that happy.

A reporter trailed them into the locker room. He went right up to Scott. "How did you do it, Champ?" he asked. "How does it feel to be a star?"

At first, Scott didn't answer. He stared at the floor. Then he spoke in a soft tone.

"You've got it all wrong," he said. "I listened to you too much. I thought you were right. I wanted to think you were right. I was too proud to see for myself."

"What do you mean?" the reporter asked.

"I'm not the star," Scott told him.

"How does it feel to be a star?"
the reporter asked.

"Someone else should get the praise. And there he is right there." Scott pointed to Lew. "He makes me look good."

In a way, Scott felt sad. But at least he had been honest — with himself, most of all.

Wild Man

"Look at that guy," said Benny. "I'll bet he eats barbed wire for breakfast. Do you think he ever smiles?"

"Quit worrying," his friend Calvin answered. "He doesn't look that tough to me."

"But you don't have to wrestle him. I

do. He'll probably kill me," Benny said.

"So he has a mean face. We can't all look like you," said Calvin. "Now go in there and pin him."

The two wrestlers walked onto the mat. They stepped inside the circle with the referee. Calvin laughed at the sight of the two boys. They were so different. Benny's opponent looked really mean. He had deep wrinkles in his face. His thick, curly hair was jet black. Dark blue veins stuck out on his arms. And, he frowned—a mean, ugly frown.

Benny was just the opposite. His thin, blond hair framed a baby face. His skin was pink and smooth. And he smiled all the time. Benny had a beautiful smile. That was Benny's problem. He appeared too kind and gentle. He didn't look as if he could beat anyone.

To make things worse, Benny judged

Benny's opponent looked really mean.

wrestlers by their appearance. If they looked mean, he expected to lose. He would stay on defense the whole match. Calvin knew Benny wouldn't last long now. He looked scared.

The two wrestlers circled and faked. Suddenly, the black-haired boy lunged low. He hooked Benny's leg with his arm and knocked him off balance.

With a thud, Benny hit the mat. The other wrestler rode him to the floor. Both boys were squirming for position.

"Reach back and grab his leg. He's wide open!" Calvin yelled. Benny didn't hear him. He stayed on defense.

Soon, the boy on top had a good hold. He worked Benny over onto his back. Benny struggled to keep his shoulders up. But he was tiring quickly.

Within a minute, he felt his shoulders sink to the floor. It was all over. Wearily, he walked back to his teammates.

"You shouldn't have lost that one. You beat yourself," Calvin said.

"I know," said Benny. "Maybe I should take up another sport."

Calvin thought for a few seconds. Then his face lit up with an idea. "What you need is a change of image. We'll start on it tomorrow."

"What are you talking about?" asked Benny.

"You'll see," Calvin said with a grin.

The next day, Benny and Calvin met at practice. "Let's get started on your new look," Calvin said at once. "Stand over there."

Benny stood and grinned sheepishly. Calvin studied him for a moment. Slowly, he walked around his friend. "Hmmmm, this may be harder than I thought. You really are clean-cut," Calvin said. Then

Benny grinned sheepishly.

he used both hands to mess up Benny's hair.

"That's better," said Calvin. "Now quit smiling. Give me more of a scowl. Look mad."

Benny pulled the edges of his mouth down. His blue eyes squeezed into tiny slits.

"All right, lean forward," Calvin said. "Shake your head like a dog fighting an old shoe. That's it! That's perfect!"

Calvin grabbed Benny by the arm. He pulled him into the locker room. They stopped in front of a large mirror.

The face in the mirror was still Benny's. But he looked wilder and tougher. Still, he couldn't help but grin.

"I feel so silly," Benny laughed.

"That's because you know it's an act. But your opponent won't know," said Calvin. "Think of yourself as an actor.

Watch some of that wrestling on television. You might get some more ideas."

Calvin didn't see Benny until the next match. He waited for him in the gym. The two teams were warming up.

Suddenly, the gym doors banged open, and someone growled. *"AAARRRGGG!"* Everyone stopped and turned to the door. Calvin's eyes opened wide at the strange sight. He shook his head and stared again. All the wrestlers were gawking. Benny stood by the open doors, beating his chest with his fists.

With a yelp, he leaped inside. He wore a bright red robe covered with plastic jewels. A long, fake scar was glued to his cheek. A flowing, white scarf hung around his neck. And his hair was no longer blond. It was dyed flaming orange. Under his arm, he carried a thick board.

With a yelp, Benny leaped inside.

"*AAARRRRGGG!*" Benny growled again. He took a few more steps into the gym. Then he stopped and shook his head wildly.

With a yell, Benny raised the board above him. Suddenly, he jerked it straight down. The board landed square on top of his head. It broke in half.

Benny gave an evil cry. Snarling and snapping, he walked over to Calvin. Calvin pulled him to the side.

"Well, what do you think?" Benny whispered. Calvin was speechless. "I did what you said," Benny continued. "I watched some wrestling on television. That's where I got the idea for the hair. The board trick was my own idea. I cut it most of the way through earlier. Do I look wild enough?"

Calvin burst out laughing. "More than wild! You went too far. You're a walking joke. But it's too late now. Your match is about to begin," Calvin answered. "Go get him, Wild Man!"

Benny threw off his robe. His opponent was waiting. To Benny, his opponent looked very tough. But Benny could appear tough, too. He shook his head and screamed. The other boy began to laugh. When he laughed, he didn't look tough anymore. That was all Benny needed to see.

Benny lunged in and got a hold. The laughing boy was down in an instant. He struggled to escape. Benny twisted him over on his side. Another shove rolled him on his back. Benny put pressure on the boy's shoulders. They finally touched the mat. Then Benny jumped up with a shout. He had pinned his man in no time. He danced back to the bench.

"You'll have to use that act in every match," Calvin said.

"No, it'll never work again," Benny panted. He and Calvin glanced over at the other wrestling team. Some of them were still laughing at Benny. But the boy who had lost wasn't even smiling. He looked angry and embarrassed.

"You're right," Calvin said. "It won't work on him again."

"That's O.K.," Benny answered. "For all I know, he's just acting, too. He sure wasn't as tough as he pretended to be."

Long Arm

"Is Frank coming to play?" Gary asked.

Beside him, Tim was dribbling a soccer ball with his toe. "He said he was," Tim answered. "But don't expect too much from him. He hasn't played a lot of soccer. He's quick, but he's clumsy."

"That's O.K. We need one more player. Then the teams will be even. But we can't wait much longer," said Gary. He looked at the other team. They were kicking around an extra ball.

"Here he is now," Tim called. He pointed down the street.

It was Frank all right. Even from far away, they could pick him out. Everything about Frank was long. His feet were long. His arms and legs were long. Even his face was a bit long. He was the tallest boy on the field.

Basketball was Frank's best game. Still, he enjoyed all sports. He was glad Tim had invited him to play.

"I hope I didn't hold you up. I had an errand to run," called Frank.

"No problem," Gary said. "We were just about to begin."

"Where do I play?" Frank asked.

"I'll start out as goalie," Tim replied. "You stay up front with Gary. Score a

"Here's Frank now," Tim called, pointing down the street.

few goals for me."

"We'll try," Frank and Gary answered.

Seconds later, the ball was in play. Gary was a good soccer player. He moved the ball downfield with his feet. He kicked it along as he ran. His teammates spread out across the field.

The other team tried to stop the attack. Two players moved in on Gary. They planned to steal the ball. Quickly, Gary kicked it over to Frank.

Frank charged toward the goal. The ball rolled along at his feet. Two defenders rushed at him. Frank started to pass back to Gary. But suddenly, his feet tripped over the ball. Frank fell over on his face. And the ball rolled right to his opponents.

The other team raced it toward Tim. Frank scrambled to his feet, but he was too late. Tim was outnumbered. He tried to guard the goal. But he couldn't prevent the kick. The ball zipped past him. Frank saw it skip into the net.

"Sorry about that," Frank called. "My feet got tied up."

"It happens to all of us," Gary said. Tim kicked the ball downfield.

Again, Gary led the attack. He booted the ball across the field. His teammate tapped it along for a few yards. Then he passed it back to Gary.

Gary looked for a man near the goal. Frank broke into the open. He cut across the middle. At once, Gary knocked the ball to him.

Frank had a wide, clear shot. He drew his foot back for a powerful kick. He swung his leg with all his might. But his toe never hit the ball. It struck the ground first. And Frank landed back on his face.

Frank's toe never hit the ball.

A while later, the boys took a rest. By then, Frank had lost the ball seven times. Gary stopped Tim on the sidelines. "We've got to do something about Frank," he whispered.

"What do you mean?" Tim asked.

"He's killing us. He has two left feet. Every time he touches the ball, he trips. He falls right over it," said Gary.

"I warned you not to expect a great player. He's new to the game," Tim answered.

"Let's put him in another position," Gary said.

"Where? Soccer is a running game," Tim told him.

"Not for the goalie," Gary said with a smile.

"It's worth a try," Tim answered. "But I still don't expect much."

Frank was happy to change positions.

Tim followed him to the goal. "Stop the ball as well as you can. And use your hands," Tim said. "That's the goalie's extra weapon."

"At least I won't have to run," Frank laughed.

The game started up once more. Frank stood ready in front of the goal. He watched the action and waited.

Tim and Gary controlled the ball. They passed it back and forth between them. They worked it downfield. Their footwork was smooth and sure. They made it look easy.

Suddenly, Tim tried to score. He kicked the ball hard and low. The goalie barely got to it. But he still saved it. Quickly, he passed it out to his teammate.

Frank crouched low and stayed ready. The other team was coming quickly downfield. They kept the ball to the left side.

Frank wondered who would take the shot. There was so much space to protect. He couldn't cover it all. But he had to try.

A second later, someone tried to score. The boy aimed his kick for the right corner. Frank leaped to that side. His body hung parallel to the ground. His long arms were stretched out far.

No one thought Frank could save it. But the ball hit right in his fingers. With a huff, he landed in the grass. Instantly, he jumped to his feet and booted the ball out to midfield.

Gary stopped it with his foot. Then he kicked it to Tim. This time, Tim's shot was on target. The ball sailed into the net. Tim threw up his arms in a wide V.

"Great save, Frank!" Tim shouted.

The pace of the game was picking up. In no time, the other team was back near Frank. Gary tried to steal the ball. But he lost his footing. When he fell, the other player had an open field. He rushed the goal and kicked hard.

Once again, Frank hurled his long body into the air. His fingers barely grazed the ball, but that was enough. The ball bounced wide.

"Beautiful job!" Gary shouted. Frank's face was one wide smile.

By game's end, Frank had made more great saves. Few shots slipped past his long reach.

"You were terrific, Frank," Tim said.

"I agree," Gary added. "The long arm ruled the goal."

"Don't forget my feet," said Frank.

"I couldn't if I tried," laughed Tim.

Ball, Strike, and Duck

"Look at that wild man throw," said Jeff. "His arm is like a slingshot." Jeff and Ken were sitting in the dugout. Neither one of them had been to bat yet.

"I don't want to look," Ken told him. "We'll see those pitches close up soon enough." Ken rose and paced back and forth. He was scared. He loved baseball. But he was afraid of being hit by the ball. That's why he didn't play in the infield. He felt at ease in the outfield. The balls had already slowed down by the time they reached him.

Soon Ken would be facing Bruce Miller. No one pitched as hard as Bruce. His fast ball was like lightning. But it wasn't always a strike. Ken just knew he would be hit. Bruce had already struck one boy today. Ken didn't want to get on base that way.

The inning ended before Ken was up. He grabbed his glove and ran to left field. He tried to forget about Bruce. Right now he had to catch, not hit.

The first batter for the Reds struck out swinging. The next one sent a long ball to Ken. He stepped under it and

Bruce's fast ball was like lightning.

caught it. The third batter knocked a grounder to second base. The throw to first was high, and the man was safe. Another pop fly sailed over third base. Ken charged in and dove head first. The ball landed in his glove.

"Great catch!" Jeff called. They trotted to the dugout. "Get ready because you're up after me."

Ken hated to leave the field. He practiced his swing while Jeff batted. His friend went for the first three pitches. And he missed them all. "That ball is really flying," he told Ken. Ken wished he hadn't said that.

Slowly Ken stepped up to the plate. He was sure his knees were knocking. He was also sure Bruce knew he was scared. The pitcher grinned from the mound. Ken wanted to close his eyes.

Bruce began his wind-up. The ball shot

41

out of his hand. It zipped right for Ken's helmet. The batter fell into the dirt.

"Ball one," said the umpire.

Ken stood up and brushed himself off. *The next one's going to get me,* he thought. He stepped back into the batter's box.

Bruce started his wind-up again. Ken got ready to jump out of the way. The baseball came in like a rocket. Ken leaned far away from it.

"Strike!" the umpire shouted. The pitch had been right down the middle. But Ken was too scared to see it.

He'll tag me for sure this time, Ken said to himself. He stood as far from the plate as he could. Again, Bruce threw a burning strike. Ken never even saw the last pitch. He was just too nervous. Bruce didn't even throw it that hard. It was a perfect strike. Ken could have hit

Ken fell into the dirt.

it, but he didn't swing.

For the next few innings, Ken was in a fog. He caught what came to him. But he was thinking of other things. He was mad at himself. The pitcher was just using him. Ken stepped up to the plate twice more. And each time, Bruce did the same thing. His first pitch was wild and fast. After that, Ken was too scared to swing at anything.

Other players were getting hits. By the last inning, the score was tied, 4-4. The Reds did nothing with their final bat. Ken and Jeff ran together to the dugout. Jeff would be batting second. And Ken would be up after him.

"Here's our chance," Jeff told Ken. "We're acting like rookies out there. He's not that good a pitcher. We're just too shaken up to hit the ball. Let him think you're scared of him. Then he'll throw those easy strikes."

They watched the first batter at the plate. The boy planted his foot and lifted the bat. Bruce let loose with a wild curve. The batter tried to twist to the side. But the baseball kept curving in. It smacked his shoulder with a thud.

"I didn't need to see that," Ken moaned. His teammate was rubbing his bruised skin.

"Take your base," the umpire called. The batter jogged down to first base.

"That's one way to get on," Jeff joked. "I hope to do it with less pain. Remember what I said about staying calm." He walked into the batter's box.

Ken saw Bruce smiling at the new batter. He wound up and threw a screamer. It brushed by Jeff's waist.

"Ball one, inside," said the umpire. The next pitch was not as hard. It, too, was a little close to the batter. "Ball two, inside," came the call.

Bruce laid the third pitch down the middle. Jeff swung for all he was worth. The baseball cracked off the bat. It sailed deep into right field. The man on first waited and watched. When the ball was caught, the runner took off. He rounded second and headed for third. The throw from the right fielder was off. The runner was safe on third base.

Jeff came back to the dugout happy. "Remember what I told you, Ken," he said. "Keep your nerve, and he'll pitch to you. The winning run is on third. All you need is a hit. Go get him."

Ken knew that Jeff was right. But that didn't make it any easier. Bruce was still out there grinning. Ken didn't have to pretend he was scared. He really was afraid.

The first pitch is the one to watch. Just don't let it rattle you, Ken told himself. He stepped up to the plate.

Bruce wound up and let go. The ball flew right under Ken's chin. He jerked his head back. "Ball one, high and inside," the umpire said.

Ken backed out of the batter's box. He looked over at Jeff, who was leaning out of the dugout.

"Now he'll really be pitching!" Jeff said to Ken. "He thinks you won't swing."

Ken moved back to the plate. He didn't want to swing. He wanted to stay as far as he could from the plate. But he made himself move in close. Ken was going to swing. It didn't matter what the pitch looked like. He had to try.

Bruce hurled the ball to the catcher. Ken swung the bat level. *Crack!* The ball

Ken swung the bat level.

shot straight back at the pitcher. He might have caught it. But he ducked out of the way. Ken grinned all the way to first base. The winning run crossed the plate.

The Eye
of the Basket

Dave stepped up to the foul line. The official handed him the ball. Slowly, Dave bounced it three times. His eyes were glued to the basket. He was trying to block out the noise in the gym.

These next two shots were so important. The Hawks were down by one point. They needed just one basket to tie the score. That would send the game into overtime. But if Dave made both shots, the Hawks would win.

The gym roared with yelling fans. Dave squinted at the rim. He raised the ball and slipped it off his fingers. The shot was inches to the right. The crowd groaned as the ball spun out.

Dave's head fell onto his chest. He backed away from the foul line. With deep breaths, he calmed his nerves. He shouldn't have missed that easy shot. Now he *had* to make the next one.

Again he took the ball. He edged his toes to the line. As before, he bounced the ball slowly. His heart was pumping madly. The ball arched off his hand. It landed on the lip of the basket. And then it fell to the side.

The other team shouted with joy.

The ball arched off Dave's hand.

They jumped up and down beside their bench. The Hawks walked sadly toward the locker room. But Dave still stood at the foul line. He stared at the basket. How could he have missed both shots? At last, he shook his head and turned away.

"You sure blew it," someone called from the stands. Dave pretended that he didn't hear the remark. But the voice would always stick in his head.

The locker room was very quiet. No one spoke as they showered and dressed. They had wanted this game badly. And they should have won it. Dave sat by his locker and stared into space.

"Hey, don't worry about it," said Hal. He had the locker next to Dave's. "We all have our bad games now and then."

"How about a bad season?" Dave sighed. "I haven't been on yet. You should have heard the wisecracks from the stands."

"You know how fans are," Hal said. "They all love you when you're a winner."

Hal tried to encourage Dave. He wanted to say more. But the coach's voice drowned him out. "Dave, come in my office," the coach shouted.

The other players watched Dave step inside. The door swung shut behind him. Dave braced himself for a lecture. But it never came.

"Well, what's the problem?" asked the coach. He spoke in a low tone. "Last year, you burned the net right off the basket. Now you can't make anything but a lay-up. Do you feel all right?"

"I feel fine," Dave told him. "I've just lost my aim. I know exactly what I'm shooting for. But the ball goes somewhere else. I really am trying. That's the truth."

"I can see that," said the coach. He chewed on his whistle for a few seconds. "Maybe some extra practice would help. I'll meet you down here tomorrow. We'll see if we can't solve your problem."

"Thanks, Coach," Dave said. He was surprised the coach hadn't yelled. Quickly, he slipped out the door.

The next day, Dave was at the gym early. He was warming up when the coach arrived. The coach fed him the ball. Dave tried a shot from every spot on the court.

First, he took long jumpers from the corners. He would dribble and plant his feet. Then he would leap with the ball above his head. At the peak of his jump, he would shoot. The ball would fly in a high arc. Sometimes, it would zip through the net. But more often, it would hit the side of the rim. After an hour, Dave's jumpers weren't looking any better. And he was feeling worse with each miss.

Next, the coach moved him to the foul line. Dave felt calm and relaxed. He wasn't under the pressure of a game. As always, he bounced the ball three times. Then he took his shot. One-third of his attempts were good. But last year, he was hitting twice that.

Finally, Dave worked on his lay-up. He would charge the basket from the foul line. Near the backboard, he would flip up the ball. Dave had no trouble making those. After a few lay-ups, the coach told him to rest. They sat together on the bench.

"I just don't know, Dave. You've got great form. But the ball lands a little off," said the coach. "We'll figure it out yet. Go check the clock in the hall. It should almost be time for lunch."

Dave looked out through the gym door. Then he began walking down the hall. His head was stretched forward toward the clock. The coach watched him with a puzzled face. Suddenly, he raced to the door.

"Where are you going?" called the coach.

"To see what time it is," Dave answered. He pointed ahead to the clock.

"Stop right there!" the coach said. Dave felt as though he were in trouble. But he didn't know why. The coach ran up beside him. "What time is it?"

"That's what I'm going to find out," Dave laughed. He started to take a step. But the coach grabbed his arm.

"You can't see the clock from here?"

the coach asked.

"I can see the clock. But the hands are a little blurry," said Dave.

"Come on," the coach said in an excited voice. A minute later, the coach was on the phone. He wrote a name and address on a piece of paper. He tossed it over to Dave. "You be there at three o'clock tomorrow," he said. "We play the Warriors at five. Get here as soon as you can."

Dave was late getting to the game. He could hear the noise in the gym as he dressed. The game had just started. He ran past the stands to the bench. His teammates didn't recognize him at first. Dave was wearing glasses.

"How do they feel?" the coach said.

"Fine," Dave answered. He leaned off the bench and looked down the hall. "It's five-fifteen."

The coach grinned. He signaled a player to call time-out. Dave went into the game.

The Hawks took the ball out of bounds. Hal threw it in to Dave from the side-lines. Dave dribbled around the top of the key. No one came out to cover him. They didn't think he would shoot from there. And they weren't worried if he did.

Calmly, Dave took the long shot. The ball soared toward the backboard. *Swish!* It zipped through the net.

Dave made three more like that in a row. The Warriors were soon coming out to cover him. And their defense was falling apart.

The game ended with a happy roar. Dave had scored twenty-five points. And the Hawks had defeated a tough team.

On the way to the locker room, the

Calmly, Dave took the long shot.

coach stopped his team. He lined the players up across the hall. "Now, is there anyone else who can't read that clock from here?" he asked. No one spoke out. "O.K., team," he said. "Now go take your showers."

Running on the Pedals

"I hate to tell you this," said the doctor. "Your running days are over." He held an X ray up to the light. Then he pressed the side of Robert's knee.

Robert jerked from the sharp pain. "You're kidding, aren't you?" he asked.

"You know that running is my favorite sport. I'm the fastest person on the track team. I run at least five miles a day."

"I'm telling the truth, Robert," the doctor said. "Your knee can't take it much more. When you run, your foot beats the pavement. That pounding will ruin your knees. Don't even walk much for the next month."

Robert left the doctor's office with a frown. He had never felt worse in his life. Slowly, he limped to the track. From the bleachers, he watched his teammates. They were running the hundred-yard dash. No one came close to Robert's speed. But it didn't matter now.

A tall sprinter walked over to Robert. "How's the knee?" he asked.

"Not very good, Brian," said Robert. "The doctor told me I have to quit running. My knees can't take the beating."

"That's a shame," Brian said. They sat staring at the track. Suddenly, Brian snapped his fingers. "I just had a great idea. My brother is on a bicycle racing team. They're always looking for good athletes. It's kind of like running. And your knees don't get jarred to pieces. I'll tell him to give you a call."

"Gee, I don't know if I want to," Robert said.

"What have you got to lose?" Brian asked. He jumped up and ran back onto the track.

For the next month, Robert just sat around. His knee no longer hurt him. But his spirits were still low. Brian's brother, Peter, came by to visit. He brought over a sleek, black bicycle. Robert rode it down the street as fast as he could. He thought his knee would get sore. But it felt fine. Still, he was unsure about joining the team.

"We're having a race next week," said Peter. "You could try your hand at racing then. I have another bike I'll ride. Just keep this one for a while."

Robert couldn't argue with that deal. He rode every day that week. Soon, he was used to the bike. He could cut turns quickly and sharply. Riding ten miles was easier than running five. And his knee didn't bother him at all.

Leaving early, Robert went to the race. He had never seen so many bike riders. The sight of them made him smile. *Some of these people are half my size. I'll blow them off the highway,* he thought. He found Peter working on his gears.

"Hi, Robert," Peter called. "We're glad you came." Robert met the other members of the team. Then Peter gave him

I'll blow them off the highway,
Robert thought.

some advice. "Don't ride too fast at the start," he said. "You have twenty miles to cover. Find someone moving at your pace. Then stay right behind him if you can. Let him block the wind for you. You'll get the idea after a few miles."

The racers went to the starting line. Peter's team was near the front. Robert rolled up right behind them. He was sure he could keep up with them. The race began with a pistol shot. The pack sped down the road.

But Robert had started off in the wrong gear. He could barely spin the pedals. In seconds, Peter's team had pulled far ahead. So had many of the other racers. Robert shifted to an easier gear. He built up speed and chased after the others. The chain whirred between his feet. And the wind whipped through his hair.

He learned a lot in those first few miles. He saw that he couldn't catch Peter. The team was too far ahead. Then Robert remembered what Peter had told him. There was one other rider nearby. He fell in behind him.

At once, Robert knew what Peter had meant. It was easier riding behind someone. The boy in front had to fight the wind. Robert's front wheel was inches from the leading bike.

I'll let him do all the work, he thought. *When we're near the end, I'll speed past.*

The two racers rode together for a long way. The leader wanted to shake Robert. He tried to jump ahead with bursts of speed. But Robert stuck right with him. This racing had become a lot of fun. Then he heard the hiss of air. At first, Robert thought it was his tire. All at once, the boy in front pulled over. He was the one with the flat.

Robert rolled on down the highway. He looked ahead for someone to follow. But no one was close. When he next glanced behind him, he saw that there was a bike right on his tail. Now Robert was breaking the wind for someone else.

He looked back again. His shadow was a smaller boy. He seemed to be much younger than Robert. And he was much thinner. Robert didn't know how long he had been there. But he wasn't going to let him stay.

With a cry, Robert bolted ahead. He dashed down the edge of the road. After a few seconds, he peeked back. The kid was still with him. His tire was an inch behind Robert's. Now Robert knew how the racer he had tailed felt. He couldn't let this runt beat him. The finish line was over the next long hill.

The kid was still with Robert.

Robert tried to outrun him again. But the youngster stuck to him like glue. Together they started up the slope. Robert shifted levers to find an easier gear. Just then, the kid made his break. He stood on the pedals and flew by. He had caught Robert off guard. Robert found the gear at last. But, by then, it was too late to catch up. The skinny rider zoomed across the finish line.

Robert found Peter resting in the shade. "You're here so soon?" asked Peter. "That's great for your first race. With practice, you could be a winner. How did you like it?"

"Fine," Robert told him. "But that little squirt over there beat me."

"That's Jimmy Sands," Peter laughed. "He's a smart racer. There's more to this than running on the pedals. Jimmy proves it by beating stronger riders."

"How did he learn?" Robert asked.

"He joined a racing team," said Peter, smiling.

Robert smiled, too. "When do we start training?"

One Hundred
Per Cent

"Try it again," Steve called. "Hold your racket at more of an angle."

Tom picked up one of the balls near him. Tennis balls were scattered all over the court. Steve was helping Tom improve his game.

Tom stepped close to the back line. He tossed the ball up with his left hand.

With his right, he swung the racket. The ball shot over the net. It flew like an arrow. It hit the ground and spun to the left.

"That's a little better," Steve said. "Turn your racket an inch more."

Tom served time after time. Finally, his arm was worn out. "That's enough for today," he shouted.

Steve began picking up the balls on his side. Tom did the same. They dumped them in a sack at the net.

"Your serve is looking stronger," said Steve. "The spin makes the ball curve sharply."

"It's still not like yours," answered Tom. He wanted to be as good as his teacher. "Yours really cuts hard when it hits."

"That's my best shot," Steve told him. "I save it for when I have to win. It catches my opponent off guard. If you know it's coming, you can return it. So I don't use it much."

"I hope I can master it. It's a great shot," said Tom.

"You will. By the way, there's a tournament next week. Why don't you enter?" Steve asked. "The competition will help you. I'm going to sign up tonight. Shall I put your name down?"

"Sure," Tom said. "I'll work on my serve between now and then."

Tom had one more lesson before the tournament. Again he and Steve focused on his serve. It wasn't anything like Steve's. Still, it was getting pretty tricky.

Steve gave him some more tips, too. He wanted to see his student do well. Tom was an above-average player. And he was improving each day. Steve hoped Tom would be in the top ten.

Tom arrived at the tournament first. Steve found him staring at a white board. The players' names were written on it. The names were matched up in pairs. Tom was laughing softly.

"What's the joke?" Steve asked.

"Oh, hi," said Tom. "I was just looking at the schedule. If we both win today, we play each other next. Isn't that crazy? I might have to play my own instructor."

"Don't think you can't beat me. You have the ability," Steve said.

"Well, I have to win today first. That won't be simple either. I play Ed Carson," said Tom.

"You can beat him," Steve told him. "I'll try to be there."

Steve won his own match easily. Then he rushed to catch Tom's match. It was nearly over. Tom needed just one point to win. He was getting ready to serve.

First, he checked his footing. Then he tossed up the ball. His racket swished over his head. *Thwack!* The ball zipped across the net. It skipped off to the left. Ed missed it completely.

Tom jumped with glee. He had won his first tournament match. Steve ran out to praise him. He was as proud as his pupil.

"I couldn't have done better myself. You were fantastic!" he said.

"That serve you taught me did the trick. It really faked him," Tom said. "He thought it would bounce right to him. How did you do?"

"I won, too," Steve told him. "We play tomorrow at noon."

Suddenly, Tom lost his smile. It came back a second later, but it didn't seem the same. "I'll see you at noon," Tom said.

Tom never had a chance for it.
He was in the wrong position.

He hurried off the court. Steve wondered why Tom was acting so strangely.

The next day Tom wasn't any friendlier. "Hello," he said simply. Then he ran to his side of the court. The two warmed up silently.

"Are you ready?" Steve called. Tom nodded.

They flipped a coin for serve. Tom won the toss. He carried two balls to the back line. He took a long, steady breath. Then he began his serve.

Steve waited across the net. He eyed the ball like a hawk. It came in low and fast.

Steve slapped the serve back hard. Tom barely got to it. He knocked it high and down the middle. Steve was already there. He drove the ball to the far corner. Tom never had a chance for it. He was in the wrong position.

Tom went back to serve again. The ball flew straight to Steve. Steve caught Tom standing on the right. He hit a powerful backhand. It flew down the left sideline. As before, Tom was in the wrong place.

Steve won the first set with ease. He didn't have to use his best shots. Tom was making all the mistakes.

The two players rested between sets. Steve stopped Tom at the net. "What's the matter with you?" he asked. "I know you can play ten times better."

"I'm just off. That's all," Tom said.

"You're more than just off. Now what's the problem?" said Steve.

At last, Tom told him. "The problem is you. I feel awkward playing you. You're my friend and my teacher. I feel funny trying to beat you here. This isn't just a friendly game. This is a tournament."

"What's the matter with you?" Steve asked.

Steve understood. "Your thinking is all wrong. Don't think about beating *me*. Try to beat my game," he said. "That's what sports are all about. Always try to play one hundred per cent. Don't hold back. Give me your best game. You won't beat me anyway." Steve winked as he walked away.

Tom trotted to his side of the court. He had his old grin back. He felt much better. And he was hungry for victory.

The boys battled hard in the next set. Tom was like a new player. No one got an easy point. Slowly, Steve pulled ahead. He was winning five games to four. He only needed one more point. Taking his time, he went back to serve.

Across the net, Tom leaned forward. He rocked back and forth on his feet. The racket was clenched in his hand. Tom knew what was coming. Steve

Steve flung the ball high.

would use his best serve now. It would spin to the left. Tom was ready to spring that way.

Steve flung the ball high. His racket sliced through the air. *Pop!* The ball took off like a rocket.

Quickly, Tom bolted to the side. The ball landed in mid court. But it didn't skip left. Instead, it veered to the right. It was out of reach. Steve won the point and the match. The players walked off the court together.

"That wasn't fair," Tom laughed. "I was expecting a left-hand spin on the ball. You've never used that serve with me."

"That's another key to tennis," smiled Steve. "Don't show anyone everything you have."

"Just wait until next year," Tom kidded. "I'll have some tricks of my own."

"Now you're talking," Steve told him.

Hot Streak

Bam! The shot echoed off the school building. Kevin rose out of a crouch. His legs strained for speed. His arms pumped through the air as he ran. His sharp cleats dug into the track. The world on each side of him was a blur.

Quickly, Kevin glanced over his shoulder. The other five runners were behind him. One was just two steps back. Together, they raced through the first turn. Kevin could almost feel the boy panting behind him.

On the straight stretch, Kevin held his position. The other runners couldn't gain any ground. Kevin led the way into the last curve. He looked back once more. Then he set his sights on the finish line.

With his head high, he began his kick. He moved like the wind. Without looking, he knew he was pulling ahead. He pushed himself as fast as he could go as he crossed the finish line.

"Way to go, Kevin!" Doug called. Kevin was leaning forward gasping for breath. Doug slapped him on the back.

Kevin raised his head and smiled. At last, he caught his breath. He shook hands with the losers. Then he sat on

Kevin moved like the wind.

the bleachers. Doug plopped down beside him.

"This makes twelve wins in a row," said Doug. "That's almost a record."

"You know why I won," Kevin laughed.

"Because you ran a good race," answered Doug. "Those smelly socks don't have anything to do with it."

"I'm not too sure about that," Kevin said. "Ever since I quit washing them, I've been winning."

"And the rest of us have been dying," joked Doug.

"Well, plan on dying some more. As long as I win, I'm not washing them. You should try it, too," Kevin told him.

"No thanks," Doug laughed. "One skunk to a track team is enough."

Kevin went to the locker room to change. He removed his dirty socks and put them with his towel. Then he went in for a shower.

As he bathed, he thought about his race. He really had run well. But he had worn the winning socks, too. At first, he had stopped washing them as a joke. Now he wasn't laughing. Maybe they did have some great power. After all, he wasn't a super sprinter, but his string of wins had now reached twelve.

I'll find out for sure Thursday, he thought as he stepped out of the shower. *Terry Taylor was faster than lightning last year. I'll see what he can do against me and my socks.* Kevin hummed as he dressed. Suddenly, he stopped cold.

Something wasn't right. He looked around the room.

Kevin dumped his track suit on the floor. The lucky socks weren't with his other clothes. He checked in his shoes, but they were empty. He hunted beneath the bench. Finally, he guessed where they were.

Kevin bolted past the coach's office. He charged into the small room beside it. "Oh, no!" he cried.

The team manager was bent over the washing machine. His arms were filled with clean, wet towels. "Need a towel?" he asked.

Kevin didn't speak. He saw a lone sock hanging from the damp bundle. The boy pulled it free. The other sock was still in the washer.

"I'm sorry," said the manager. "I must have picked them up with a towel."

"That's O.K.," Kevin sighed. "I should have put them in my locker." He looked as though he had just lost a friend.

Doug saw Kevin back out on the bleachers. "You'll never guess what happened," Kevin said. "My socks have been washed."

Doug couldn't help but chuckle. "Terry Taylor will sleep better tonight," he joked. Kevin didn't even smile. Doug stopped laughing.

"Look, Kevin," he began. "You've won the past twelve races on your own. Dirty socks didn't win them. *You* did. You can beat Taylor in your bare feet. Just run your regular race."

"I guess you're right," Kevin answered. "The socks were clean when the season started."

It seemed as if Thursday would never come. Kevin was looking forward to the race. At the same time, he dreaded it. He wanted to run against Terry Taylor. But he wished his socks were still dirty. They looked so white as he pulled them on.

Kevin went out to the track. His was

"My socks have been washed," Kevin said.

the first event. Doug rushed up behind him. "You've got him," Doug said. "I can see it in his eyes." They both looked over at Terry. He was waiting at the starting line.

Kevin took his place beside him. Other runners moved in around them. They all crouched down.

The starter raised his pistol. "Runners, on your mark! Get set!" *Bam!*

Kevin and Terry burst off the line. Their feet hit the pavement at the same time. At once, they jumped ahead of the pack. This would be a two-man contest. They both struggled to take the lead. They ran neck and neck to the first turn.

Suddenly, Terry pulled a step ahead. He cut to the inside of the curve. Kevin followed right on his heels. He didn't like to start off at such a fast pace. But he had to stay close.

The racers came out of the turn. Kevin pushed hard and moved back alongside Terry. They charged down the long straight stretch. Side by side, they approached the last turn.

Kevin searched his body for energy. He had to take the lead now. His legs strained to cover more ground. At the last second, he cut in front of Terry. The runners leaned into the curve. They shot into the final stretch.

Kevin kicked with everything he had. He sprinted to the inside lane. Now Terry would have to come around him. Kevin could feel him closing in. He summoned all of his strength and dove over the finish line.

Kevin felt as if his lungs were on fire. His chest heaved up and down. The track team swarmed all over him. "You did it!" Doug cried.

Kevin dove over the finish line.

Kevin flopped over in the grass. He pulled off his shoes and yanked off his socks. Then he headed for the trash can. Terry met him on the way.

"That was a fine race. Congratulations," Terry said.

"Thanks," answered Kevin. He was just about to drop the socks in the can.

"I look forward to racing you again. I left my lucky shoes at home. I won't forget them next time," said Terry. He waved and ran off.

Kevin's hand clutched the socks. He stepped away from the trash can. *Maybe I'll keep these just in case,* he thought. *You just never know.*